For Tobi. — CA

I dedicate this book to my family, as always.
And a little thought for Dakota. — QL

Norman, Speak!

Caroline Adderson PICTURES BY Qin Leng

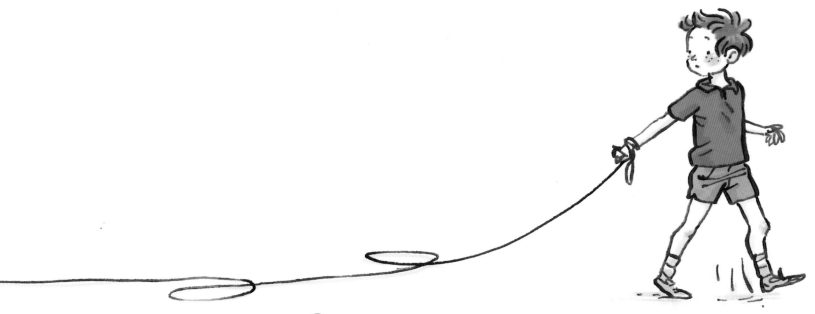

Groundwood Books House of Anansi Press Toronto Berkeley

WE WENT TO the animal shelter. So many kinds of dogs were there — brown, black, white, gray, large and small, curly and straight.

We looked at each dog in its cage, and each dog looked back. The sad way those dogs looked at us made me want to cry.

Mom asked, "Which one?"

"All of them," I said.

"Twenty-four dogs?" Dad said.

"Okay. Let's take the saddest one."

But which one was the saddest? It was really hard to tell. This one? That one?

"I know how to choose," I said.

"Which dog has been here the longest?" I asked the shelter woman.

She pointed to a brown-and-white dog. Where the other dogs had tails, this one had a stump.

"He was a stray," the woman said. "Someone found him and brought him in. No one knows his real name. Norman is what we call him."

"Norman's the one I want," I said.

Norman wagged when we opened the cage. He wagged when we left the shelter. First his stump twitched, then his whole rump swung from side to side. His wag was a hula dance of happiness.

At home, I tried to teach Norman to do dog things.

"Norman, sit," I told him.

"Norman, come!"

"Norman, speak!"

"Norman!" I called.

Norman didn't understand a word we said.
Whenever we spoke, he tilted his head and stared.
Maybe he kept forgetting his name was Norman.
Or maybe nobody had trained him properly.

But after a few days with Norman, we knew the
truth. He just wasn't very smart.

We loved Norman anyway.
"He's so funny," Mom said.
"He's so friendly," Dad said.
I said, "I don't care that he isn't smart."
What I loved best about Norman was his funny-brown-hula-stump-wiggle-wag dance. He would meet us at the door and wag all around us. Whether we were gone three minutes or three hours, it didn't matter. Norman danced.

One day a new dog came to the dog park, a black one. Norman did his funny-brown-hula-stump-wiggle-wag dance for him. Then Norman and the black dog chased each other until the owner of the black dog called out.

The black dog ran straight over to the man.
And so did Norman.
The black dog sat.
And so did Norman.
The black dog held out a paw to shake.
And so did Norman.

The owner gave his dog a treat. And he gave one to Norman, too.

We went over to the man. He was talking to both dogs, and both dogs were listening. We didn't understand a word he said.

Then he turned to us and asked, "Is this your dog?"

"Yes," we said.

He laughed. "Your dog understands Chinese. Did you know that?"

"Norman! Why didn't you say so?"

We signed up for Chinese lessons on Saturday mornings
in the basement of a church.
   "We should bring Norman," I said.
   "We can't bring Norman," Mom said.
   "Dogs aren't allowed in churches," Dad said.

Wǒ shì
Wáng Lǎoshī.

The teacher's name was Mrs. Wang. She wouldn't say a word in English.

"*Nǐ hǎo,*" she said.

"*Nǐ hǎo!*" all the kids called back.

"*Wǒ shì Wáng Lǎoshī,*" Mrs. Wang said. She pointed to each student.

"*Wǒ shì* Emily," one said.

"*Wǒ shì* Morris," said another.

Mrs. Wang pointed to my dad. He scratched his head and smiled.

"I don't understand a word you're saying," he said.

When the class was over, we lined up at the door. All the kids filed out, saying, "*Xièxie, Lǎoshī,*" to Mrs. Wang.

But when I said, "*Xièxie, Lǎoshī,*" everybody laughed.

Mrs. Wang said, "You just called me a mouse."

All the way home I practiced Chinese in my head so I could speak to Norman. We came in the door, and Norman did his happy hula wag for us. His stump wiggled. His rump swayed. I let him lick my face.

By then, every Chinese word was gone.

"Norman," I said. "You must be *really* smart."

We didn't feel very smart the next Saturday morning in the basement of the church. Or the Saturday after that. All the other kids were smarter.

We tried to learn to count. *Yī, èr, sān, sì.*

That was as far as we got.

"We're not very smart," I said.

Mom gave me a pat. "But we're friendly."

"And we're funny," Dad said. He threw a paper airplane. It landed on Mrs. Wang's desk.

All the kids laughed.

"Chinese is too hard," he said. "I quit."
"You can't," I said. "What about Norman?"

"Mrs. Wang," I said. "We have a dog."

"*Gǒu*. Dog."

"We have a *gǒu*. His name is Norman, and he only understands Chinese. He doesn't care that we can't speak it. He loves us anyway. But I'm going to try really hard to learn it."

"Not me," Dad said. "I'm not smart enough."

Mrs. Wang said something in Chinese to Dad and shook her finger at him. Then she smiled.

"More effort," she said. "Fewer jokes."

I said, "Mrs. Wang, could you teach us some words so we can all talk to Norman?"

I can count in Chinese now. I know the days of the week. And at the dog park, we all call, "*Gǒu, lái!*" And Norman comes.

We say, "*Zuòxià*," and Norman sits. He does it every time.

Then we say, "*Hěnhǎo*, Norman," and pat his head. Because he's a good dog.

We say, "*Wǒmén ài nǐ*, Norman." Because we do. We love Norman.

"What language does your dog speak?" people ask us.
"Chinese," we say.
"Chinese! It's so difficult to learn. What a smart dog!"
"He is," we say. "But that's not why we love him."

Nǐ hǎo	Hello	你好
Wǒ shì Wáng Lǎoshī.	My name is Teacher Wang.	我是王老师.
Wǒ shì Emily.	My name is Emily.	我是 Emily.
Xièxie, Lǎoshī.	Thank you, teacher.	谢谢老师.
Yī, èr, sān, sì	One, two, three, four	一, 二, 三, 四
Gǒu	Dog	狗
Gǒu, lái!	Come, dog!	狗, 来!
Zuòxià	Sit	坐下
Hěnhǎo, Norman.	Good, Norman.	很好, Norman.
Wǒmén aì nǐ, Norman.	We love you, Norman.	我们爱你, Norman.

Text copyright © 2014 by Caroline Adderson
Illustrations copyright © 2014 by Qin Leng
Published in Canada and the USA in 2014 by Groundwood Books

Groundwood Books / House of Anansi Press
110 Spadina Avenue, Suite 801, Toronto, Ontario M5V 2K4
or c/o Publishers Group West
1700 Fourth Street, Berkeley, CA 94710

The publisher would like to thank Lissa Chen for the Chinese translation.

We acknowledge for their financial support of our publishing program the Canada Council for the Arts, the Government of Canada through the Canada Book Fund (CBF) and the Ontario Arts Council.

Canada Council   Conseil des Arts
for the Arts   du Canada

ONTARIO ARTS COUNCIL
CONSEIL DES ARTS DE L'ONTARIO

Library and Archives Canada Cataloguing in Publication
Adderson, Caroline, author
Norman, speak! / written by Caroline Adderson ; illustrated by Qin Leng.
Issued in print and electronic formats.
ISBN 978-1-55498-322-3 (bound). — ISBN 978-1-55498-323-0 (html)
I. Leng, Qin, illustrator II. Title.
PS8551.D3267N67 2014   jC813'.54   C2013-904911-8
C2013-904912-6

The illustrations were done in ink on paper
and colored digitally.
Design by Michael Solomon
Printed and bound in Malaysia

FSC
www.fsc.org
MIX
Paper from
responsible sources
FSC® C012700